THE FOURTH GRADE READER

12 Short Stories for Kids in 4th Grade

CURIOUS BEE

ISBN: 979-8-89095-039-0

Table of Contents

Introduction

Stories are an excellent source of information and imagination. Fiction and non-fiction tales take us to far-off places we've only dreamed about, and they help us learn more about the world around us. Stories teach us about other cultures, countries, and places far beyond like the past, the deep ocean, and distant space. There is no limit to what stories can teach us when we read!

The stories in this book have been crafted especially for readers at the fourth-grade level; ages eight through ten. Readers will be met with the appropriate number of challenges in learning new words, building reading comprehension skills, and understanding more complex sentence structures. They are designed for independent reading, but some readers may enjoy adults reading to them!

Studies show that children who are regularly read to, have a better grasp of language including vocabulary, syntax, grammar, and comprehension. Secondly, children who hear stories frequently have more developed social-emotional skills, are better problem solvers and perform better once they start school. So don't be shy about asking an adult to read to you!

Because everyone develops differently, some of these stories may be simple to read while others may have some challenging words. Overall, however, most fourth graders reading on this level should be able to read our tales. When you come across an unfamiliar word, use context clues to decipher its meaning. If you don't own a dictionary, the fourth grade is an excellent time to buy one!

If you are in, soon to be in, or just graduated from fourth grade, this book is for you. Do your best to decode and read new words you come across using context and pictures to understand their meaning. However, there is no reason these stories can't be read to you. So, ask your favorite adult to share in the fun by reading a story or two to you!

As a bonus, we've included a list of open-ended questions you can ask yourself before, during, or after reading a story. These questions will promote critical thinking, enhance comprehension, and further develop language and literacy skills. Each story also has three to five comprehension questions specific to that tale included at the end.

We hope you enjoy reading these engaging fourth-grade stories as much as we enjoyed creating them for you!

Happy reading!

Open-Ended Questions To Ask Before, During, Or After Reading

Each of the following questions is designed to promote critical thinking, problem-solving, social-emotional skills, and language and literacy skills.

For adults reading with kids, feel free to adapt the language of the questions as needed to your child's age and developmental level and based on the story!

Questions to Ask Before Reading

1. Looking at the picture, what do you think this story is about? Why? What clues does the picture give you?
2. Based on the title, what do you think this story is about?
3. If you've read this story before, do you remember what happens in this story?

Questions to Ask During Reading

1. What do you think will happen next? Why? What clues do you have?
2. Do you agree with the characters' choices? Why or why not?
3. How do you think the story will end? Why?
4. What could (the character) do differently?
5. What would you do if you were in this situation?

Questions to Ask After

1. Before we started, you said you thought the story was about (blank). Were you correct? Why or why not?
2. Did you enjoy this story? Why or why not?

3. What was your favorite part of the story? Why?
4. What was your least favorite part of the story? Why?
5. Can you think of another story you know that is like this one? What do they have in common? What is the difference between the two?
6. Who was your favorite character? Why?
7. Do you think the characters solved the problem well? Why or why not?
8. How would you have solved the problem in this story?
9. Was the story fiction or non-fiction? How do you know?
    a. Fiction means made up or not real.
    b. Non-fiction means a true story.

The Magician's Apprentice

Chapter One

Muriel was a magician's apprentice. Being an apprentice meant she was learning to be a magician; she was not one yet. But almost. Tonight, was her first performance as a magician. Muriel was in her third year of studying to be a magician under The Great Mossimo!

The Great Mossimo, whose name was really Mortimer Sussman, was one of the most famous magicians in the country. For years he traveled all over the country, performing his shows in packed theaters, carnivals, fairs, and festivals. But Muriel had first seen the Great Mossimo when she was only six years old at the Queen Victoria Theater in the center of the city.

Her father had taken off work from his job at the shipyards on a Saturday afternoon to take her to the show. The show was marvelous. The Great Mossimo levitated, multiplied one flower into a dozen, cut a woman in half and put her back together, and escaped from a series of chains in a locked box! Muriel had never seen anything so amazing; she knew right then that she wanted to grow up to be a magician.

But when she told her father she wanted to be a magician, he only smiled and said, "Only men become magicians, little one; maybe you can be a magician's assistant one day!" Muriel didn't want to be an assistant, but what her father said was true. She had only seen male magicians. "Perhaps I'll be the first!" Muriel said. "Perhaps you will," her father replied," with a smile on his face.

That was 20 years ago. Muriel's father was now retired from the shipyard, and she had left the city with The Great Mossimo eight years ago on her quest to become a magician!

Chapter Two

It was not entirely by accident that Muriel met the Great Mossimo, although he believed it was. Alongside the performance announcements for The Great Mossimo's show was a notice that said he needed a new assistant. She was determined to get that position so she could begin learning the secrets of magic.

Muriel had been seeing his show every year when he came to the city. Sometimes, her father went with her, but sometimes he had to work, so he bought her a ticket and she went alone.

The night Muriel met The Great Mossimo, or Mortimer as she would eventually call him, he had just finished his Saturday night performance in the city. Muriel had observed him the last few nights and knew he always went to the Greek restaurant two blocks from the theater after a performance.

She stood on the corner, in the shadows, waiting for him to exit through the theater door. When he did, she quietly followed him from the shadows. She watched him enter the restaurant and take his regular seat at the counter. Muriel waited a few more minutes, then walked into the restaurant and sat two seats from The Great Mossimo.

Of course, he no longer looked like the Great Mossimo in the restaurant. He wore a faded pair of trousers, a blue denim shirt, and a hat pulled down over his ears. He sat sipping a cup of coffee. If Muriel hadn't seen him perform every year for 12 years, she would have never recognized him outside of his costume and away from the stage lights.

She pulled out the book she had brought, *Lessons from the Great Houdini,* and tried to read. She was too nervous to actually read, but she pretended to, hoping he would notice her book.

Chapter Three

Muriel placed the book on the counter with the title facing up as she ordered a sandwich and soda. She hoped Mossimo would look over, see her book, and then begin talking to her, but he only stared into his coffee.

After several minutes, she realized she needed another way to get his attention. Muriel accidently dropped her book on the floor. In the quiet restaurant, it made a loud bang. The book landed right at Mossimo's feet.

"Oh, I am so sorry!" Muriel said, getting up to retrieve her book.

"It's Okay. Let me get it," Mossimo said, reaching down for the book. As he picked it up, he noticed the cover. "You like magic?" He asked her.

"I *love* magic!" said Muriel. "I am trying to learn as much as possible about it. Do you like magic?" She asked him, pretending not to know who he was.

"Yes, I enjoy magic," he said, sitting back down. "There's a magician in town right now, The Great Mossimo. Have you ever heard of him?" He asked Muriel.

"Of course!" Muriel said, "I've been watching his shows since I was six; he's wonderful. He's actually the reason I became interested in magic."

"Is that so?" Mossimo asked her. "I know him, and he's looking for a new assistant; maybe you should audition."

"Me?" Muriel asked, "well, I could. I've seen his shows, but I don't know how he does any tricks."

"Well, I know The Great Mossimo," he said about himself, "and most people don't know much before they start. But I know he will train the right assistant when he finds them. Why not audition?"

"Well, maybe I will!" Muriel said, excited her plan had worked. "Do you know when the auditions are going to be?"

"Sure do!" He said. "Tomorrow at 9 a.m. at the Queen Victoria Theater. Knock on the stage door when you arrive and tell them that Mortimer sent you, that's me," he said, reaching out his hand.

"I'm Muriel," she replied, shaking his hand. "A pleasure to meet you, Mortimer."

Chapter Four

The following day, Muriel was outside the stage door at 8:55 a.m. She knocked on the door and waited. Several minutes later, an elderly man with stooped shoulders opened the door.

"Hello," Muriel said, "I am here for the magician's assistant audition; I was told to say Mortimer sent me."

The man squinted his eyes and looked closely at Muriel. He stared at her for several seconds, then opened the door wider. "Come on in," he said. "Take those stairs up two flights, and you'll be in the wing of the stage."

Muriel did as the man directed. Three other young women were waiting when she reached the top of the stairs.

The tallest one had blonde ringlets and rosy cheeks like apples. She looked at Muriel, nodded a hello, but didn't speak. The second was shorter than Muriel and had long black hair almost down to her waist. She looked incredibly nervous. The third girl was about Muriel's height and had glossy, wavy brown hair. She looked at Muriel, "Hi! I'm Helen, nice to meet you!"

Muriel replied with a quiet hello and asked what they were waiting for.

The girl with the long black hair said, "We're waiting for the Great Mossimo to appear, then we're supposed to walk on stage."

As soon as she finished speaking, there was a puff of smoke, and on the stage appeared The Great Mossimo! "Ladies," he said, "please come onto the stage!"

The girls walked out.

"I am the Great Mossimo! Thank you for coming today. You have all been asked here by my friend Mortimer because he saw something special in you. I will teach you all the same trick, and then you will perform the trick for me."

Muriel was nervous but thought it sounded easy enough. The girls learned the trick and then, one by one, performed as The Great Mossimo sat in the audience. Muriel wondered if any other girls knew that Mortimer and Mossimo were the same person.

Once they had all completed the trick, Mossimo asked them to take a seat. "Ladies, thank you for coming today. It was a tough decision as all four of you performed the trick well. But I have decided my new assistant shall be…, Muriel!"

Muriel jumped out of her seat. "Really?" She said. She couldn't believe it!

The other three girls quietly congratulated her and then left the theater.

Mossimo told her they would leave the city at 6 p.m. sharp that night. He told her to return home, gather her belongings, and meet him at the theater door no later than 5:45 p.m.

Muriel promised to be there and ran home to tell her father.

Chapter Five

When Muriel returned that evening, she saw Mortimer waiting at the door. She continued to pretend she didn't know that Mortimer was, in fact, The Great Mossimo. "Hello, Muriel!" He said, "and congratulations!"

"Thank you," she said. "Where's Mossimo?"

"Ah, about that..., I am Mossimo."

"You *are*?" Said Muriel, feigning ignorance.

"But I have a feeling you already knew that," Mortimer said. "It's not every day young women interested in magic show up at the same restaurant as me."

Muriel smiled. "Well, I admit I did want to meet you - magic is my dream!"

"I am happy you are joining me. I will begin teaching you on the train and at every stop we make until you are ready to perform. It will be quite an adventure!"

And what an adventure it was. Muriel learned everything she could from Mortimer, his old assistant Betty before she left to move to California and other magicians they met along the way. After five years as his assistant, Mortimer told Muriel he wanted to retire, and he needed to train a replacement; he offered the job to Muriel.

She accepted and began studying more complicated solo tricks. Three years later, she was about to perform her first show - with

Mortimer as *her* assistant! She gave herself the name Mystical Magnolia. She was nervous but ready.

And the best thing of all was that sitting in the front row of the theater was her dad, who had taken her to her very first magic show all those years ago.

Reading Comprehension Questions For *The Magician's Apprentice:*

1. How old was Muriel when she first watched the Great Mossimo perform? How many years had she been his apprentice by the end of the story?
2. Why do you think The Great Mossimo introduced himself as Mortimer at the restaurant? Why didn't he tell Muriel who he was?
3. Do you think Mortimer meant to pick Muriel all along as his assistant? If yes, then why did he make the other women audition?
4. How do you think Muriel felt the night of her first show as the magician? Why?
5. Why do you think Mossimo/Mortimer chose Muriel to be his assistant?
6. Do you think Muriel became a famous magician? Why or why not?

Did George Washington Ever Tell A Lie? And Other Presidential Folk Lore

Chapter One

There is a myth that says George Washington never told a lie. The story goes that at six years old, he was given a hatchet as a present. Young George took the hatchet and cut down his father's favorite cherry tree. Then, when his father confronted him and asked him if he had cut the tree down, the story tells us his response was, "I cannot tell a lie; it was I who cut down your cherry tree."

Every historical record tells us that this story is untrue. There is no proof it ever happened. Yet, the tale continues to be passed down, and many people believe it to be true. In fact, many stories we hear about famous people in history are inaccurate, missing details, or one hundred percent untrue. So, how do stories like this begin? Where did Washington's story start? And what other presidential legends exist that are not based on fact? Let's find out!

Chapter Two

The story of George Washington and the cherry tree was started by his first biographer, Mason Locke Weems. A biographer is a person who writes the life story of someone else. Weems was also a publisher and bookseller. His goal when writing about Washington was more about selling books and making money than telling the truth.

It seems odd that someone would make up stories and lies about a real person, but it has happened throughout history and happens today. If you hear or read news about celebrities, they are not always true. People enjoy hearing interesting, seemingly impossible, and shocking stories about famous people. So, journalists and other news sources that create these stories often embellish or add details to make them sound more interesting.

George Washington died in 1799, and by early 1800, the biography by Weems titled *The Life of George Washington with Curious Anecdotes* was published. It became an instant best-seller. Weems was not worried about telling an actual account of Washington's life; he knew what readers wanted to read. Washington, the great general and first president, helped lead America to independence from Great Britain. The American people saw George Washington as a hero, and Weems knew people wanted to read stories that made Washington sound like a hero.

The cherry tree myth wasn't the only myth Weems wrote in his book, but it became the most famous. It is so famous that people still believe it is true today!

When other authors wrote about George Washington, they used Weems's biography as a source. Therefore, many other writers told the tale of Washington and the cherry tree. Over time, the story changed slightly and was embellished or added to; that is how a myth or legend is created. People also like the story about Washington, and it is nice to believe that our great American general, hero, and president would never tell a lie. And while George Washington may have been an honest man, the next time you hear someone tell the story of the cherry tree, you will know it is a made-up tale!

Chapter Three

Another newer myth about a larger-than-life American president is based on a photograph circulating the internet in the early 2000s. It's a photograph that showed Teddy Roosevelt, our 26th president, riding a giant moose in a lake!

Teddy Roosevelt is famous for being a big game hunter who often traveled to Africa to hunt exotic animals like lions, cheetahs, and crocodiles. During his presidency, he brought many unique pets to the White House, including a bear, a lizard, a pig, a badger, a blue macaw, and a hyena, to only list some. Therefore, it is easy to imagine Roosevelt riding a moose!

However, the picture, first published in 1912, was fake. It was published as part of a political advert during the presidential campaign. In 1912, Roosevelt ran against the current Republican president, William Howard Taft, and Democratic candidate, Woodrow Wilson, who would win the election and become president in March 1913.

Teddy Roosevelt was president from 1901–1909. At the time of his presidency, he was a Republican. He was followed by William Howard Taft, who was also a Republican. When Roosevelt decided to run in 1912, he created a new political party called the Bull Moose Party.

The original ad showed Wilson riding a donkey, the political symbol for democrats; Taft riding an elephant, the Republican symbol; and Roosevelt on a moose to symbolize his new party.

Nearly 100 years later, the picture of Roosevelt on the moose became an internet meme and instant legend. However, the myth was quickly de-bunked because of the number of historians that saw the photo and better historical records today than in Washington's time. However, it is fun and easy to imagine the 26th president riding a moose near a lake!

Chapter Four

Another popular myth about another very famous president is that the 16th president, Abraham Lincoln, built the log cabin where he grew up all by himself. This myth is so famous that there is even a popular toy you may have played with called Lincoln Logs!

Again, like our other presidential myths, this one is easy and fun to imagine. But if you stop and think about it for a minute, you will realize this could not be true! How could Abraham Lincoln build the house he grew up in? He could not have built it as a baby or a child. So, where and how did this myth start?

This one is much easier to trace to its source. Abraham Lincoln grew up in a log cabin; that part is true. He was born inside the cabin his father built on February 12, 1809, in Hodgenville, Kentucky. But he did not grow up inside that cabin.

Log cabins are so connected to the 16th president that a log cabin is inside a marble monument marking his birthplace. But the cabin on display differs from the one in which he was born. The cabin on display was built by businessman Alfred Dennett and his business partner James Dingham using logs they found near Lincoln's rumored birthplace.

In 1897, the cabin was toured around the country as an attraction for people to view. People believed this to be the cabin where Lincoln was born. While it was on display on Coney Island, some of the logs were mixed with the cabin known as the birthplace of Confederate President Jefferson Davis.

When the cabin returned to Kentucky in 1906, it was recognized as a representation of the cabin where Lincoln was born, not the actual building.

When Lincoln was two, his family built a second log cabin near Knob Creek Farm in Kentucky. Then again, in 1816, his family moved to *another* log cabin in Spencer County, Indiana. Lincoln stayed in Spencer County for another 14 years. He likely helped his father, Thomas Lincoln, a skilled carpenter, build cabins for other people. It often took several men to build a cabin.

It is easy to see how this myth was formed and why people so easily believed that Abraham Lincoln could build a log cabin by himself!

Chapter Five

There are many stories about presidents, athletes, warriors, queens, kings, and others throughout history. Some stories are positive, and we want to believe them because we like the person they're about. Likewise, believing negative tales about people in history or celebrities we do not like is easy.

However, when you hear or read an amazing tale about someone, do your own research to discover if it is true. You'll learn other interesting facts along the way while discovering if the story you heard is true.

This lesson should be applied to regular people in our lives, too. When you hear a rumor or story about a friend, teacher, teammate, or another person you know, especially if it is negative, don't simply believe it. Ask questions and talk to the person to discover the truth!

The presidents in these three stories aren't alive to tell us what's true, but our friends and family are. So, the next time you hear a crazy story, be a history detective and discover the truth!

Reading Comprehension Questions For *Did George Washington Ever Tell A Lie? And Other Presidential Folk Lore:*

1. The word "lore" is used in the title. Now that you have read the story, what do you think the word "lore" means? What context clues did you use?
2. Why do you think people find it so easy to believe stories they hear or read about famous people?
3. The story is non-fiction, but it still teaches a lesson. What is the lesson you think the story is trying to teach?
4. Name three facts you learned from this story.
5. Think about a story that you've heard about someone famous. Conduct some research to see if you can discover if the story is true or not.

The Weaver In The Sky

Chapter One

Once upon a time, there was a beautiful and intelligent princess. The princess lived in a palace as beautiful as she was, perched high on the mountaintop. The princess had many talents. When she sang, her voice sounded like a nightingale. When she drew, her pictures looked like they'd come to life straight off the page. She was always the fastest or strongest when she competed in sports competitions. And when she sat at her loom and wove, she created the most beautiful and softest fabric anyone had ever touched or seen.

The princess's mother, the queen, was neither mean nor jealous of her daughter's beauty and talent. In fact, she was quite proud of her daughter, but the queen rarely let her daughter leave the palace. Because her daughter was gifted with superior beauty and talents, she feared others would become jealous of her and try to harm her. Occasionally people were allowed to visit the palace for festivals or competitions, but the princess was always carefully watched.

The queen had heard tales of a wicked old crone who lived deep in the woods below. The stories said the old crone stole beautiful and talented maidens so she could have their beauty and talent for herself. No one knew what happened to the girls afterwards because they were never seen again.

But no one had seen the crone in the witch's lifetime. Still, the occasional maiden from the city below would disappear, and it was always rumored to be the old crone who took her. In the past month, five girls from the city had disappeared.

The queen knew the only way to keep her beautiful and talented daughter safe was to keep her inside the palace.

Chapter Two

Around the same time that the five girls went missing in one month, it was also time for the annual Primrose Festival. The Primrose Festival was the princess's favorite event all year. The most talented artists, musicians, and performers from the entire kingdom came to the city during the festival. It was also one of the few times the princess was allowed to leave the castle each year.

So, when the queen told the princess that she would not be able to attend this year, she cried and begged her mother to let her go. The queen told the princess it was for her safety, but she didn't care.

Once her tears slowed, she told her mother she had an idea. What if this year they held the festival *inside* the palace walls? Could she go then? The queen thought that this was an excellent idea. She immediately began preparing for the festival to be inside the palace walls.

On the first morning of the Primrose Festival, the princess hopped out of bed. She dressed quickly and ran to the main hall. The princess has secretly entered one of her weavings into the tapestry competition. She did not want the judges to know it was her weaving, out of fear they would pick her just because she was the princess. The weaving contest would be judged in one hour, so the princess, followed closely by her guards, walked around the festival listening to music and looking at other art pieces.

When the tapestry competition was about to begin, the princess, with a hood pulled up to hide her face, stood in the crowd and watched. The judges announced the third-place winner, a fishpond filled with colorful fish and plants; the winner climbed onto the stage to accept her prize. Then they announced the second-place winner, an intriguing weaving of a battle. The weaver accepted his prize, made a small bow to the crowd, and then left. Then, the judges revealed the first-place winner, the princess's tapestry, a beautiful tapestry of a pink and gold sunset. The sunset was so realistic it was hard to believe it was fabric.

When no one climbed onto the stage to accept the prize, the judges called out for the winner, but they had no name. Reluctantly, the princess took down her hood and climbed on stage. The people gasped. Very few had seen the princess in person. The princess graciously accepted her prize and climbed down. Waiting at the bottom of the steps was the man who had won second place. He told her he had never seen such beautiful weaving before and asked her to show him how it was done.

The princess agreed to give him lessons, and they started that very afternoon!

Chapter Three

The man's name was Haruto, which means spring or sunny person, and that is precisely what he was. The princess learned that he was a guard who worked inside the palace. He had just started working a few months before the festival and had never met the princess. The two quickly became best friends, and she taught him everything she knew about weaving.

As the months passed, there were no new reports of missing girls, so when the winter festival approached, the queen allowed the princess to attend as long as Haruto and her regular guards were with her.

The winter festival's theme changed yearly; this winter, the theme was *Ice Dreams*. There were ice sculptures and frozen treats to eat. There was an ice-skating rink located in the center of the city. Everything glistened and sparkled.

The princess and Haruto decided to ice skate. While Haruto went to find skates, the princess noticed a silvery twinkle down a side street. She wondered what it could be; it was so beautiful. When her guards turned their backs, the princess slipped away down the street toward the twinkle. When she was close, she saw it was a star carved out of ice floating in the air. She wondered how this was possible and reached out to touch the star. The exact moment she touched the star, the princess disappeared.

Chapter Four

When the princess woke up, she didn't know where she was. She couldn't feel her body, and she saw darkness and small twinkling objects all around her. She tried to move, but there were no arms to wave or legs to kick. She could see, but did she have eyes?

Then she heard a voice. The voice sounded as if it came from all sides at once. It told her she was now part of the sky; she had become part of the stars.

"You were so lovely, and your weaving was so beautiful, I had to have you for my collection," the voice said.

The princess tried to speak but found she had no voice. The voice told her that her job was to weave beautiful tapestries out of the sky's lights, colors, and stars to create sunrises and sunsets for Earth.

"Think about what you want to weave," the voice said, "and imagine you are pulling the colors toward you."

The princess did as the voice said, and slowly, she saw purples and pinks mixing together; she added a deep orange and wisps of white.

"Excellent!" The voice said quietly.

The princess watched as her sunset moved across the sky and slowly descended to the earth. It seemed to float to the other side of the world, far from where she lived.

"Now weave me more sunsets like your beautiful tapestry so I can use them in the sky tonight."

Back in the city, Haruto and the princess's guards searched everywhere for her. It seemed as if she had simply disappeared. But that was impossible! How did a person disappear?

As the sun began to set, Haruto felt despair. The princess had been lost when she should have been safe with him! He sat down on the ground and looked at the sky. As he watched the sunset form, an odd feeling came over him; the sunset in the sky looked exactly like the princess's tapestry from the Primrose Festival. But it couldn't be, could it?

Haruto raced back to the palace to the room where the princess kept all her tapestries. He held the weaving up to the sky. It was a perfect match! Before disappearing, she had made dozens of sunset tapestries.

So, each night, Haruto watched the sunset form and found the tapestry that matched one from the princess's weaving room. The princess never returned, and no one ever saw her again. Still, each night, the sky glowed in remarkable colors that always matched one of the princess's weavings.

Reading Comprehension Questions For *The Weaver In The Sky:*

1. Do think it was fair for the queen to keep the princess in the palace all the time? Why or why not?
2. Do your parents have any rules that you don't think are fair? What are they? Why don't you think they're fair?
3. Who do you think the voice in the sky was? Why?
4. What do you think happened to the other girls that went missing?
5. How do you think the princess felt realizing she could never go back to Earth?
6. What do you think happened to Haruto after the story ended?

Freddy's Family Farm

Chapter One

Freddy's family farm had belonged to his family for as long as anyone could remember. The farm was started almost 150 years ago by his great-great-great-great-great grandfather in 1749. A sign out in the front told everyone who visited how old the farm was. The sign read: *Jameson Family Farm, Established 1749.*

Freddy also knew this because his father and grandfather had taught him. They told Freddy that one day, the farm would belong to him and his sister Ruth, so it was important that he learn everything he could. Freddy was even named for his ancient grandfather, Frederick Adam Jameson.

Freddy loved his family's farm. They grew corn, potatoes, pumpkins, and apples. Every fall, they had a large pumpkin patch and hayrides, and people could visit and pick their own pumpkins or head out to the orchards to go apple picking. And in the summer, they grew big juicy watermelons and strawberries.

Freddy loved the animals they had, too. There were free-range chickens who laid fresh eggs which they sold in the family farm store and goats whose milk Freddy's mom turned into soaps, lotions, and other bath products. They even had four cows whose milk they used to make fresh, delicious ice cream that they sold.

Freddy loved everything about the family farm. The only problem was Freddy didn't want to run the farm when he grew up. Freddy wanted to be a dentist.

Chapter Two

It might seem odd that a young boy wanted to be a dentist, but Freddy found teeth fascinating. He had watched a TV special a few years ago and started learning everything he could about teeth. He also wanted to help people. He knew the farm helped people, but he wanted to help them in another way.

The problem was Freddy didn't know how to tell his family.

Freddy's family had run the farm for so long that he couldn't be the one to disappoint everyone! He wondered how Ruth felt about running the farm; she was a few years younger than him, so maybe she didn't know either. All Freddy really knew about Ruth was that she loved pigs. Ruth spent a lot of time helping her uncle, who also worked on the farm, in the petting zoo area.

Freddy's dad had been the first person in his family to attend college. His dad studied agriculture and business. College is where his dad met his mom; she studied accounting. Freddy's mom had never been on a farm before she met his dad, but now, 15 years later, when you looked at her, you would think she had grown up on one, too.

Freddy had never told anyone in his family how he felt because he was nervous that they would be upset. He went to school, got excellent grades in math and science, and took piano lessons. He had chores on the farm, which he enjoyed doing; he just didn't want to be in charge of the farm.

Freddy didn't know what to do, but he would be starting high school the next year and wanted to apply for the specialized medical science prep program.

He knew he had to make a decision soon.

Chapter Three

The months passed, the school year continued, and Freddy kept up his chores on the farm. During the winter, Freddy often worked in the family farm store after school when there was less work outside. The winter was also the slowest month at the farm and store. The chickens always laid eggs, and the cows and goats needed milking daily, but nothing grew outside. Although there was some work to prepare the fields for the spring, his dad, his uncle, and the hired farm employees did most of the prep work.

His mom had recently started experimenting with a greenhouse and growing flowers and plants. However, it was still new, and little had grown so far.

Freddy spent his extra free time reading books about dentistry, teeth, the mouth, and general books on the body and health. At school, he loved his biology and health classes the most.

One morning in February, Freddy's principal announced there was going to be a science fair at the high school. This year, they would allow eighth graders to enter a project for the first time. Freddy became very excited. He didn't know what his project would be yet, just that it would be about teeth.

He took the permission slip home and asked his parents to sign the form. His father asked him if he wanted to do a project about animals and livestock.

Freddy said he wasn't sure. His mom asked him if he wanted to use her new greenhouse to do a project on plants. He told her he wasn't sure. His sister told him he should experiment with butterflies, but he told her he definitely wasn't doing that.

Freddy read books about animals and plants. He read about other experiments done on teeth and mouths. He took notes and made diagrams. After several weeks of research, he decided what his experiment would be!

He told his mom and dad he wanted to use the cows to experiment with their diet. He didn't tell them the experiment was to discover which plants were healthiest for the cow's teeth. He told them he would not feed the cows anything dangerous but didn't want to discuss the experiment until he had his results.

His parents trusted him since he had grown up on the farm and worked and fed the cows for years. Plus, they used less cow's milk in the winter and early spring because the homemade ice cream shop was closed until May. So, if anything the cows ate affected their milk supply, it would be okay. His parents were proud of him for entering the science fair and told him they were excited to see what his experiment taught him.

Chapter Four

Over the following month, Freddy fed each of the cows a different diet of plants he had researched. One cow he kept on her regular diet; this was called the control. It meant nothing was changed or different about this cow. He added carrots and broccoli to the second cow's diet and into the third cow's diet, cabbage and cauliflower. For the fourth cow, he added turnips and zucchini to her diet.

Freddy kept detailed notes on the cows' energy levels, milk production, and overall teeth health. When their farm veterinarian, Dr. Ramos, made her monthly visit to check on the animals, Freddy asked her several questions about a cow's mouth and teeth. He explained his experiment to Dr. Ramos, and she thought it was a fantastic idea! She told Freddy to call her if he had any other questions.

The week before the science fair, Freddy's dad drove him to the store to purchase the items he needed to create his display. Freddy's dad asked him how the experiment went, and Freddy replied that he was happy with the results. But Freddy wouldn't tell his dad anything else. Freddy's dad wondered what this mysterious cow experiment could be but didn't ask any more questions. He knew Freddy would tell him when he was ready.

Freddy worked secretly in his room the following week to assemble the science fair display. On the morning of the fair; his mom helped him load his materials into her car and drove him to the high school. She dropped him off and told him the family would return at noon once the fair was officially open.

Freddy set up his experiment in the Life Sciences section of the fair. He was very proud of his project. He had photos and diagrams and close-up pictures of the cows' teeth, which were funny!

The judges walked around an hour before the fair opened to the families. They awarded first, second, and third prizes in each category. To Freddy's surprise, his project won second place in Life Sciences! The judges told him they were impressed with the detail and planning he put into his project.

When Freddy's family arrived, he stood proudly beside his display with the large, red second-place ribbon. His parents quickly congratulated him and then examined his display. His parents were also impressed with Freddy's research but asked why he picked cows' teeth.

This was his chance. Freddy took a deep breath and poured out everything he felt about teeth and dentistry. He told them he loved the farm but did not want to run it and that his dream was to become a dentist. His parents listened quietly to everything he said. His mom and dad glanced at each other and then smiled.

Freddy's dad told him he did not have to run the farm if he did not want to; he could still own the farm and be a dentist and hire someone else to run the farm. In fact, his dad said, his grandfather, Freddy's great-grandfather, did that exact thing. He explained that Freddy's great-grandfather was actually a barber! He ran a large barber shop in town and hired a manager to run the farm. Freddy was astounded; he had no idea anyone in his family had *not* run the farm. His sister piped up and said that perhaps *she* could run the farm! Everyone liked the sound of that.

Freddy's parents told him that what was most important to them was that he and his sister were happy. He should never be worried or scared to share his dreams and ideas. Freddy felt so much relief after telling his family about his dream. He understood that he could love the farm but also love something else. Next week, applications will be handed out for the high school medical science prep program. Freddy planned to be first in line to hand in his form!

Reading Comprehension Questions For *Freddy's Family Farm:*

1. What did Freddy want to be when he grew up? Why was he worried his parents wouldn't like his idea?
2. Describe Freddy's science fair experiment.
3. Why did the judges tell Freddy he won second place in Life Sciences?
4. Do you think Freddy was upset he didn't win first place? Why or why not?
5. Name some of the things Freddy's family grew and or sold on his family farm.
6. What job did Freddy's great-grandfather have?
7. Who was Freddy named after?

My Teacher Is A Troll

Chapter One

Some children don't like their teachers and call them horrible names like witches or monsters. My teacher is a troll. And I don't mean that he is mean or gross. I don't mean that he is big and hairy, although he is. My teacher is an actual, real-life troll!

You might be wondering how this is possible; trolls don't actually exist, do they? Well, I am here to tell you that they do. Not only do trolls exist, but contrary to legends and stories, they are pretty pleasant and intelligent. Well, most trolls are pleasant, but like all groups, there will be some mean and nasty ones. Thankfully, my teacher is not one of the mean ones!

My teacher, the troll, came from a family of trolls that lived deep in the forests. His cousin had once been confused with Big Foot! But everyone knows that Big Foot doesn't exist. Well, at least I don't think Big Foot exists…, but until a few months ago, I didn't know trolls existed either!

My troll teacher is called Mr. Horax. He is seven feet tall, has bumpy green skin, and a lot of silver hair. There is silver hair on his head, silver hair on his arms, and silver hair on his feet; I know this because he doesn't wear shoes. He says he cannot find shoes big enough for his feet, and since they don't wear shoes in the forest, he sees no reason to start now! He does, however, wear brown khaki shorts and a button-down shirt to class every day. I have no idea where he finds clothing big enough to fit him, but he does.

I WAS VERY NERVOUS when I first heard my fourth-grade teacher would be a troll. But I think Mr. Horax is the best teacher I've ever had!

Chapter Two

My first thought upon learning my fourth-grade teacher would be a troll was that he would be mean, hairy, and stinky. The hairy part, I got correct. But he is never mean and smells pretty nice, like lemons and apples. He told us all trolls smell like plants and flowers. I bet his troll town smells terrific!

I was also worried a troll teacher would give us extra homework. But Mr. Horax says traditional homework is a waste of time. He says that being outside, playing, and spending time with our family is much more important than sitting and doing worksheets. But, since the school requires *all* teachers to assign homework, Mr. Horax is very creative!

One week, our homework was to go for a walk and make a list of the different plants we saw. Another week, he asked us to play a game with our family. It didn't matter what the game was as long as it had counting and adding. My family played Monopoly! I didn't win, though; my brother Adam always wins. Somehow, he always manages to buy Boardwalk! But it was still fun, and we both beat my dad!

Another time, our homework was to go to a live music performance or a play and write a review. That worked out perfectly because my cousin Charlene was the Wicked Witch in her high school production of *The Wizard of Oz.* A lot of my friends came to see the play too. Some kids were scared of Charlene, but I wasn't because I knew she was just my cousin. Plus, her green makeup made her look a little like Mr. Horax, which was pretty neat!

But our best assignment yet was last week. Our assignment was to work with a partner and develop a new sport. The sport could be anything we wanted as long as we included the rules, equipment, and instructions on how to play. My partner, Vincent, and I came up with what we called Water-Balloon Baseball. It involved a lot of water balloons, a foam bat, and at least three two players. Hopefully, this summer, we can try it out ourselves!

But the homework assignments aren't the only great thing about having a troll for a teacher. Because Mr. Horax told us in two weeks, we are taking a field trip to the troll town where he grew up. The other fourth-grade classes must be so jealous!

Chapter Three

In the day leading up to the field trip, Mr. Horax teaches us everything we need to learn about trolls. It is fascinating learning about a culture different from my own! He teaches us some troll words. For example, "Brueix Floath" is how you say, "Good Morning." And "Munchaw" is "Thank You."

Mr. Horaz also teaches us how to separate myths and legends about trolls from what is true. For example, while trolls like to live under bridges, they don't eat people or animals who try to cross them nor ask for riddles to pass.

In ancient times, trolls asked for riddles because they believed they were brighter than all other creatures. Plus, they just really like riddles. But today, troll law doesn't allow them to prevent people or other trolls from passing if they can't answer a riddle.

He tells us he doesn't live under a bridge. He lives in a duplex on Maple Street next to a family with three kids and a dog named Buster. But his aunt Mergeth lives under a bridge!

The class also learns about ancient troll kings and queens, where trolls live today, and common troll foods. We learn how to play a troll children's game called "Pum-Porth," which involves jumping on one leg blindfolded.

Most of the class is not very good at Pum-Porth, but playing is fun!

We loaded onto a school bus the morning of the field trip as if this were any other field trip. But we all know it is not. This trip is special, not only because we are visiting a troll town but because the only way to get there is by using magic!

Our parents had to sign two permission slips. The first slip gives us permission to visit the troll town, and the second slip gives us permission to travel by magic. My dad is chaperoning because he said there was no way he was missing an opportunity to travel by magic!

Once everyone is loaded onto the bus, it is time to go. Mr. Horax explained that we would drive about 30 minutes to the entrance of a nearby wooded area.

Then, we would take a path into the woods where the magic portal was. He said you needed a troll to see the portal; that's why trolls could stay hidden from people for so long.

Chapter Four

We've reached the troll portal! All I see are a few logs on the ground, but Mr. Horax assures us this is the right place. He tells all of us to stand between two logs. Once everyone is between the two logs, Mr. Horaz picks a flower from the ground. There is a shimmering light, and everything looks a little hazy like it does on a scorching summer day.

Then, in front of us, we see the troll town. We are standing on top of a small hill that slopes downward.

"Let's Go!" Mr. Horax says, and we all follow him.

Our first stop is at a troll bakery. There, we watch a baker make a special troll treat called Kampers. Then we all get to eat one! Kampers remind me of a jelly doughnut with a pie crust. Our next stop is Troll City Hall. There, we meet the mayor of the troll town and learn about the troll government. Our third stop is the troll school, where we meet troll kids! Because trolls age more slowly than us, the kids in troll fourth grade are 30 years old! That's almost as old as my dad! But they don't look or act like human 30-year-olds. Together, we play a game of Pum-Porth, which the troll kids all win. Then we teach them how to play freeze tag, and we win that game because trolls aren't very fast.

The last stop of the day is Mr. Horax's childhood home, where his mom and dad have cooked us a traditional troll dinner. We sit around a giant troll table and hear stories about Mr. Horax as a child.

When the meal ends, we walk back up the hill out of the troll town and back to the portal. We pass through the portal and board the bus to return to school. As we drive, we all talk to each other about our exciting day!

If you had told me last year in third grade, that I would have a troll teacher, I would have never believed you, or I would have been terrified. But the school year is only half over, and it's been the best. I am proud to say my teacher is a troll!

Reading Comprehension Questions For *My Teacher Is A Troll:*

1. What would you think if you found out your teacher is a troll?
2. What did the narrator tell us about trolls and bridges? Can you think of a fairytale that has a troll living under a bridge?
3. Why did the narrator like learning about troll culture?
4. Describe what Mr. Horax was like both physically and in his personality.
5. What's a culture outside of your own that you've learned about? What did you learn?
6. Is there a culture or country you'd like to learn more about? Why?

Why Picasso Went From Blue To Rose

Chapter One

Pablo Ruiz Picasso was born October 25, 1881, and died April 8, 1973, at the age of 91. Picasso is one of the most famous artists that have ever lived. And he was a lucky artist because, unlike many others, he was famous while he was alive! Picasso is most famous for his paintings. However, he was also a sculptor, printmaker, theater set designer, and ceramicist.

Picasso was born in Spain and his father was an art professor who taught drawing. Like his father, Pablo Picasso was gifted in art from a young age. At the age of ten, he began officially studying art with his father. Picasso lived and studied for many years in Spain's capital city, Barcelona. At the age of 18, Picasso traveled to Paris, France for the first time. Paris is often considered the art capital of the world, especially for painters.

In Paris, Picasso was inspired by the color and style of French Impressionism, especially by the artist Vincent Van Gogh. He spent several years moving back and forth between Barcelona and Paris.

Picasso is considered influential because he created many different modern styles of art. Most notable is cubism, which he invented with fellow artist Georges Braque. Picasso is also famous for two periods of paintings that focused on color: the Blue Period and the Rose Period.

Chapter Two

Picasso focused on blue between 1901 and mid-1904. It was later given the name the Blue Period because blue was the main color that he used to paint during those years. Some of Pablo Picasso's most famous paintings are from his Blue Period. Paintings from the Blue Period include *The Old Guitarist, The Greedy Child,* and *Woman with Folded Arms.*

Picasso was very depressed during his Blue Period. One of his best friends had died and he felt very sad. During these years, Picasso spent a lot of time alone. He did not go out and see friends very often, but he continued to paint and create art in the monochrome hue of blue and blue-green.

Many of the paintings of Picasso's Blue Period depict sad people. He painted children, women, and men. During the Blue Period, he often painted women with children and solo people. He also often painted blind people during this time.

As the Blue Period ended, Picasso moved into what is known as the Rose Period. The paintings of this period, in contrast to the Blue Period, are colorful and cheery. So, what happened that made Picasso change his color scheme and style of work?

Chapter Three

The Rose Period was two short years from 1904–1906. In addition to using bright and cheery colors like red and orange, Picasso also began experimenting with different styles of painting. But what happened that made the painter suddenly switch from the sad blues and greens of the previous period to reds and oranges?

The switch from the Blue Period to the Rose Period wasn't an all-at-once event but happened gradually throughout 1904. Picasso made some new friends during this time as he lived among other artists and painters in Montmartre, Paris. Many historians say his relationship with Fernande Olivier may have been a prime reason for the shift.

Fernande Oliver was a French artist and model. She frequently modeled for Picasso's art, and he painted more than 60 portraits of her!

In addition to becoming friends with other painters, he met writers, poets, and performance artists who also influenced him and his art. Picasso's solitary and sad-looking figures in his Blue Period paintings changed to clowns, acrobats, and other entertainers.

Two of Picasso's five highest-selling paintings come from the Rose Period: *Young Girl with a Flower Basket* and *Boy with a Pipe.* Although the paintings from Picasso's Blue Period are more famous, his work during the Rose Period had a larger impact on modern art.

Art historians also say that the Rose Period was heavily influenced by the French style while the Blue Period was more influenced by the Spanish style.

Chapter Four

During Picasso's Rose Period, in addition to influences from entertainers and other artists, he was heavily inspired by Iberian Roman sculptures, plus Oceanic and African art.

Primitivism is a style of art that focuses on ancient cultures, or primitive times. Picasso's artwork during the Rose Period was followed by his African Period, which featured primitivism centered around the power and energy of non-Western cultures.

Primitivism became popular because the early 20th century was a time of industrialization and exploration.

White-European cultures were coming into contact more and more with native cultures. These interactions sparked an interest in the people, their culture, and their art.

During the Rose Period, Picasso also began experimenting with primitivism. His interest in primitivism took him to the next stage, which focused on tribal cultures. His experimentation with primitivism also partially led to the invention of cubism, the style of painting for which Picasso is most famous.

During the Rose and African Periods, Picasso began experimenting with shape and human form in his paintings. He combined elements of primitive art and El Greco and Renaissance art, mainly Michaelangelo.

These artistic experiments eventually turned into cubism.

In cubism, the objects in the painting are broken down into lesser shapes and drawn or painted in abstract forms. In a cubist painting, the viewer can tell what is being depicted but a person's head may have the shape of an oval or their body might be a rectangle.

Chapter Five

Whether blue or rose, realist or cubist, there is no doubt that Pablo Picasso's works are among the most influential of the 20th century; perhaps in all of art history. Picasso's paintings are displayed at museums worldwide. You can see Picassos in London, New York City, Berlin, and Washington D.C. The best places to view Picasso's art, though, are Switzerland, Spain, and France.

Many of Picasso's artworks travel around the world in temporary displays so that as many people as possible can view this astounding artist's work. Some displays stay a few weeks, some for several months.

Picasso's work is studied by artists and students globally. Few artists have shifted and experimented with style as much as Pablo Picasso. If you viewed one of his earliest paintings next to one of his last, you probably wouldn't believe they were by the same person!

His unique styles are what set him apart as an artist. Picasso was also fortunate enough to become famous as an artist while he lived. Many painters create their entire lives and never receive recognition.

Despite becoming one of the most famous artists of the 20th century, Picasso didn't sell most of his artwork. It is estimated that Picasso created more than 50,000 paintings but only sold about 8,000. Picasso was able to do this because he could sell each painting at a very high price.

A Picasso painting today is considered priceless by some art historians. However, should a Picasso painting come to auction, expect to spend $60 million or more to take it home!

Whether you agree his art is worth millions of dollars or not, there is no argument that Picasso's artwork changed the path of modern art.

Reading Comprehension Questions For *Why Picasso Went From Blue To Rose:*

1. Besides painting, what other types of art did Picasso create?
2. How old was Picasso when he started studying art? Who was his first teacher?
3. Choose one of the paintings from Picasso's Blue Period and make a drawing or painting based on the title. Then, look up Picasso's painting and compare and contrast your picture with his.
4. The word "monochrome" is used when discussing Picasso's Blue Period. What do you think "monochrome" means?
5. Describe the difference between Picasso's Blue and Rose Periods.
6. What makes Picasso different as an artist from other painters?

Waking Beauty

Chapter One

The story of Sleeping Beauty is rather famous. A beautiful princess is cursed by an evil witch and then spends 100 years asleep until a handsome prince comes along to wake her up and break the spell. There are many versions of the story. Some versions have dragons or trolls, most have fairies, and all of them have a lovely princess who takes a very, very, long nap.

But I am willing to guess that you haven't heard the tale of the 'Waking Beauty'. Unlike her fellow princess, Waking Beauty could never fall asleep. She tossed and turned night after night. She was often cranky and rude.

This story is her story and like most fairy tales this one begins "Once upon a time, in a kingdom far, far, away." But that is where the similarities end. So come along with me as I tell you the story of the tired, but true princess, Waking Beauty.

Chapter Two

Waking Beauty was not her real name. Her real name was Princess Beatrice Evelyn Marie Katherine. Princesses always have very long names; I don't know why. Her mother and father ruled the kingdom, which stretched for miles and miles as far as the eye could see.

To the north of her kingdom was a hot, sandy desert. On the other side of the desert, there was a land of fairies and witches where few had ever traveled. To the south was a mighty ocean. No one knew what lay on the other side of the ocean for no one had ever dared to cross it. To the west of her kingdom was a great forest where trolls, ogres and other creatures who loved the dark and damp woods lived. And to the east were majestic mountains so tall you couldn't tell where they ended and the sky began. Sometimes the clouds covered the top of the mountains, and it was easy to imagine the mountains went on forever.

When Princess Beatrice was a baby, her mother and father proclaimed to all four corners of the land what a wonderful baby she was. She smiled and laughed, and always slept the whole night long. Princess Beatrice grew up and became an intelligent, beautiful, and kind princess; but then she stopped sleeping.

Without sleep, the princess became surly and mean. She snapped at the servants and talked back to her parents. She was nasty to her younger brother Prince Edward and never wanted to play with him anymore.

As the days, weeks, and months passed, Princess Beatrice was unable to sleep and her lovely looks faded. She stopped reading her favorite books and refused to learn new things. She did not want to draw or paint anymore. And she refused to practice the harp or listen to music.

The palace servants would gossip about the princess's behavior to each other and then to their families. Soon, the entire kingdom knew that their princess was turning into something of a monster. Because the princess had once been lovely and kind, the kingdom began calling her Waking Beauty behind her back as a joke.

No one understood why the princess could not sleep so no one could solve the problem. The princess became more depressed and grumpier with each passing day. It seemed there was no hope she would ever sleep again.

Chapter Three

One morning after another night of not sleeping, Princess Beatrice was slumped at the breakfast table.

Her mother, the queen, entered the room and said, "Beatrice, you have not been able to sleep for several months. Your lack of sleep is making you and everyone else in the kingdom miserable. It is time we find an answer to this problem."

The princess looked at her mother through bleary eyes and asked, "But how can we find an answer? You've asked every scholar, doctor, nurse, medicine woman, wizard, and witch within the kingdom and no one can discover why I can't sleep!"

The queen replied, "It is time we search for the answer beyond our kingdom's borders. I am sending one emissary to each of the four areas surrounding our kingdom. Hopefully one of them will return with an answer or a solution."

Beatrice sat up, a little more awake than she was a moment ago. "But what if they *don't* return? No one has ever traveled the ocean before. The mountains are so tall, how could anyone climb them? And the desert between us and the kingdom of witches and fairies is so long and hot."

The queen told the princess that each emissary had volunteered and been carefully selected based on their skills, knowledge, and bravery. She said each one would carry with them magical supplies from the kingdom's most powerful witches and wizards. They would also pack herbs and medicines from the best medicine women. And they had studied everything known about these lands from the top scholars in the kingdom.

"All we can do is hope," said the queen.

Chapter Four

That very afternoon the four emissaries gathered at the palace gate with their supplies. The powerful witch 'Gossamer the Glorious' would cross the desert to the north to visit the land of witches and fairies. The sailor, and boat captain, 'Barry the Brave' would head out south on the ocean to see what he could discover. To the west into the forest went 'Gregor the Great', a mighty warrior who was half-troll, to visit his relatives and seek their wisdom. And 'Margo the Magnificent', one of the top scholars and adventurers in the land, would attempt to scale the mountains to the east.

Each brave scout bowed to the queen, king, and princess and set out on their quest.

Many weeks passed and none of the emissaries had returned. The queen began to grow anxious. While it wasn't common, people had traveled to the land of witches and fairies before and into the forest. The queen thought that Gossamer and Gregor would return for sure! But after a month, she started to lose hope.

After 47 days, a cry came from the palace walls! In the distance, they could see Gregor approaching the castle. He looked bruised and worn but he was walking. Gregor climbed up the palace steps and met the queen.

"Your Majesty," he said, "my troll cousins were not kind, however, after many battles to demonstrate my strength, they shared with me this sleeping potion said to make even the greatest beast sleep." Gregor presented the queen with a small bottle. "Give the princess two drops in a glass of warm milk."

That evening the princess drank the potion and was hopeful she would finally sleep. She slept for only one hour. But that was more sleep than she had in months. However, Gregor had warned the queen not to give more than two drops because the potion could become deadly if too much was taken.

The princess continued to take two drops with her milk and slept for one hour per night for the next three nights. Then 50 days after the emissaries left the kingdom, they saw Gossamer the witch flying toward the palace.

"Your Majesties," Gossamer said with a bow. "I am sorry it has taken me so long to return. The witches and the fairies of the north required I share one of my secret spells with them in exchange for their magic. The spell took many weeks to prepare."

"What have you brought back?" The queen asked.

Gossamer pulled a plant from her bag. The leaves were green and glistened like emeralds, and the petals of the flower changed colors like a rainbow.

"The princess should take a petal from this plant every night and rub the oil from the petal onto her forehead so she can sleep. Each night the plant will bloom again so there will always be petals."

That night the princess tried the plant and the potion, and she slept for three hours! The kingdom was overjoyed!

Chapter Five

For several more weeks, the princess took her two drops of troll potion, rubbed the witch's plant on her forehead and enjoyed her three hours of sleep. She was slightly less grumpy but still not her old, friendly self.

Then, on day 91, Margo the Magnificent returned. She told the royal family that she climbed halfway up the mountain to discover a land of talking mountain goats. They were very friendly and kind and begged her to stay and visit with them. Finally, when it was time to return home, they gave Margo a large jug of their milk. They said the princess should drink two ounces every night.

The goats told Margo to recite a spell when the jug was empty. They wrote down the spell and told her to recite it while tapping the jug three times. Then she should turn it clockwise three times and it would magically refill.

So, the princess used the goat milk with her troll potion, and the witch's flower, and she slept five hours! It was the most sleep she'd had in nearly a year!

Each morning that Princess Beatrice woke up having slept five hours, she became kinder and more beautiful. She began reading again and did not snap at the servants nearly as much. She would occasionally get out her sketchbook and draw a picture. She would not practice her harp but allowed music to be played around her.

Then on the 101st day, Barry the Brave returned. He was excited and told the story of a magical kingdom under the ocean where mermaids lived. His ship had crashed in a storm, and they saved him and nursed him back to health.

When Barry told them of his quest, the king of the mermaids had gifted him a magical shell that plays music and the sounds of the ocean.

That night Princess Beatrice drank her potion of goat's milk, rubbed the flower petal upon her forehead, and placed the musical shell next to her bed. She slept for eight full hours!

Every night, the princess followed her routine and every day, she felt better and better. The cause of her sleepless nights was never discovered, but Beatrice used her magical items to ensure she always slept well.

Princess Beatrice returned to her kind, intelligent, and lovely self and the kingdom rejoiced that Waking Beauty could finally sleep!

Reading Comprehension Questions For *Waking Beauty*:

1. Why did the people of the kingdom start calling Princess Beatrice "Waking Beauty"?
2. Choose one of the areas that surround the kingdom to the north, south, east, or west, and describe what you think it looks like. Draw a picture of the area.
3. The queen says she is sending "an emissary" to each area beyond the kingdom to search for answers. Based on the context of the story, what do you think an "emissary" is?
4. The story never tells us why the princess couldn't sleep. Why do you think Waking Beauty couldn't sleep?
5. What does Princess Beatrice think of her mother's plan to send the emissaries out for help? Does she think it will work? Why or why not?

Matthew Meets Tahoma

Chapter One

Matthew was in fourth grade. And this year he was starting at a new school in California. Matthew was born in Georgia, on the East Coast of the United States. He had lived in Georgia his whole life! But his dad got a new job on the other side of the country in California, so his family moved to their new home a week ago.

Matthew still had two more weeks until school started. So, on this sunny, bright, morning, he decided to explore his new neighborhood. His mom told him there was a park nearby, and his school was a short walk, only five minutes. He and his family had visited his new school last week.

Mathew was excited and nervous about starting at a new school. He missed his friends back in Georgia. He missed the basketball court down the street from his family's old apartment. He missed playing video games with his cousin Andrew who had only lived a few blocks away. He even missed grumpy Mrs. Corrado, who sat on her stoop and yelled at all the kids for being too noisy.

Matthew stepped outside into his new neighborhood. His neighborhood in California was very different from his one in Georgia. In Georgia, he lived in the city. There were apartment buildings, offices, stores, and schools everywhere. In California, his family had their own home with a small backyard. He liked the idea of having his own yard; his dog Ruby liked it too!

There were also many tall trees in California and the ocean was only a short drive from their house. In Georgia, he lived about an hour from the Atlantic Ocean, but here it was the Pacific Ocean. It looked and smelled different to Matthew.

In Georgia, he had to take a city bus to school. In California, he would walk to school. His school was also much smaller than his one in Georgia. Things were certainly very different on the West Coast than on the East Coast!

Chapter Two

Matthew stepped out his new front door and looked around. To his right, he saw some hills with houses perched on them overlooking the ocean. To his left, he saw the long, winding street that slowly went downhill toward his school. The air smelled fresh, a mixture of pine and ocean water. He definitely enjoyed the smell here more than that of the city!

Matthew began walking toward the school. There was a playground at the school, and he also had to pass the school to get to the park. He carried his basketball with him so he could shoot some hoops at the school net.

Matthew enjoyed his walk through his new neighborhood. Here it was mostly houses. He passed one small convenience store and looked inside as he walked by; he saw shelves with snacks, a drink fridge, and a lottery machine.

As he walked, he noticed some houses that had business signs out front. A small blue house had a sign that read *Maisie's Hair Salon.* He also saw a yellow house advertising doggy daycare, and a white house with a sign saying *David Foster, Realtor.*

He thought it was cool that people could run businesses out of their homes. His dad had to drive 45 minutes to his new office and his mom had found a part-time job at the library two towns over.

The ground leveled out as Matthew reached the school and he started to dribble his basketball. Matthew loved playing basketball and hoped he would meet friends here who liked to play too! As he approached the school basketball nets, he heard the sound of another ball dribbling. Matthew rounded the corner and saw a boy about his age shooting hoops.

Chapter Three

Matthew stopped dribbling and watched the other boy for a few minutes; he was really good. As Matthew started walking toward the nets, he called out, "Hey."

The other boy turned around, nodded at Matthew and said, "Hey!" back to him. Then the boy turned back around and started shooting hoops again.

Matthew walked over to another net and did the same. After 15 minutes, the other boy walked over to Matthew.

"Hey," he said again, "you're pretty good. Want to play together?"

"Sure," Matthew said, shrugging. Secretly, Matthew was excited this boy wanted to play with him. It would be nice to have a friend before the first day of school. "I'm Matthew," he said.

The other boy said, "Cool, I'm Tahoma. Nice to meet you."

Mathew thought Tahoma was a really cool name, but he had never heard it before. He didn't want to look or sound uncool, so he just said, "Cool."

Matthew and Tahoma played basketball for another hour before Tahoma said he had to go home. "Want to play tomorrow?" He asked Matthew before he left.

"Yeah, sure," Matthew said, "Same time?"

"That works," Tahoma said, "See you later!"

Matthew watched Tahoma walk away and then played a little bit longer. When he got home it was lunchtime and his mom was getting ready to go to her job at the library.

"Well, what did you find today?" She asked him.

Matthew told her about meeting Tahoma and their plan to play again tomorrow.

"That sounds great! Tahoma, is an interesting name, did you ask him what it meant?"

"No," Matthew replied.

"Hmmm," his mom said, "It sounds Native American, maybe I can discover something at the library today. Your sister is in her room so let her know if you need anything and I'll be home around five. I made you a PBJ sandwich and put it in the fridge."

Matthew's mom kissed the top of his head and went out the door to work.

Chapter Four

When Matthew's mom returned home from her job at the library, she told him she found a few possible meanings for Tahoma's name. She said it was definitely Native American, but it could mean a few different things all connected to water.

One meaning was "water's edge." Another was "frozen water." And a third was, a "snow-covered mountain." She told him that the Puyallup tribe called Mount Rainier, Tahoma. Matthew had read about Mount Rainier before they moved to California. It was about 600 miles north of them in Washington. He had asked his parents if they could take a trip there someday.

Matthew thought it was pretty cool to have the name of a mountain! He didn't really know anything about Native American culture. He had learned a little bit about the First Thanksgiving at school and the Cherokee and Choctaw tribes that are native to Georgia. But he had a feeling their culture was very different from the Native Americans in California.

Matthew's family was originally from Nigeria, but his parents were both born in the United States. He had traveled to Nigeria one time to visit his mother's grandmother, and he knew how different African American culture was from Nigerian. He wanted to learn more about Tahoma's culture but didn't know how to ask his new friend.

The next day Matthew met Tahoma again after breakfast to play basketball. He noticed Tahoma wearing a necklace under his shirt. The necklace looked like a fish. Matthew pointed at it. "That's a cool necklace," he said.

Tahoma looked down at his shirt. "Thanks," he said. "My grandad gave it to me."

"What is it?" Matthew asked.

"It's the symbol for my tribe, the Puyallup. I was born in Washington, but my dad moved us down here for his job at the beginning of summer."

"Me too!" Matthew said. "Well, I'm not from Washington," he laughed. "I'm from Georgia, but we just moved here for my dad's job."

"Cool," Tahoma said. "I've never been to the East Coast. What grade are you in?"

"Fourth," Matthew said. "You?" He asked, hoping it was the same.

"Me too!" Tahoma said.

The boys both smiled.

"I haven't really made any friends yet," Tahoma said. "It's just me, my dad, and my older sister. So, I'm glad you came."

Matthew felt warm and happy inside. "I'm glad I came too! I have an older sister too, but she always hides in her room on the phone! Maybe you can teach me what you've learned about California and Washington and your tribe, and I can teach you about Georgia and the East Coast!"

"Sounds like a good trade!" Tahoma said and put out his hand for a fist bump.

Matthew fist-bumped his new friend and smiled.

"Come on!" Matthew said. "You need to teach me how you do that one fancy shot."

Then the boys began dribbling again and raced back toward the basketball hoops. Both Matthew and Tahoma felt happy they had met.

Reading Comprehension Questions For *Matthew Meets Tahoma:*

1. What are some of the differences between where Matthew lived in Georgia and his new home in California?
2. How did Matthew feel when Tahoma talked to him? Why?
3. What are some things Matthew and Tahoma have in common?
4. How do you think Tahoma felt when he saw another kid playing basketball? Why?
5. Do you think Matthew and Tahoma stayed friends after the school year started? Why or why not?

Way Up In The Sky; Our Galaxy And Beyond

Chapter One

Have you ever looked up into the sky and wondered what was up there? You can see the moon glowing, the stars sparkling at night, and the sun shining during the day. You know that the planets that make up our solar system are up there: Mercury, Venus, Mars, Jupiter, Saturn, Uranus, Neptune, and the tiny dwarf planet Pluto. But from way down here, the planets we can see *when* we can see them, look like stars.

But there is so much more in the sky than just the stars, the moon, and the planets. To begin, our planet isn't the only planet with a moon. Mars has two, Neptune has 14, Uranus has 27, and Jupiter has 80! And, if you think 80 moons is a lot, Saturn has 83!

Imagine looking up into the sky and seeing 83 moons; it is probably an amazing site! The biggest moon in our solar system is Ganymede, it is roughly the size of the planet Mercury and belongs to Jupiter. Jupiter also has an ocean moon Europa. It is estimated that Europa has twice as much water as Earth, but the water is frozen.

Saturn also has two ocean moons. One of the moons, Titan, also has rivers and lakes made up of ethane and methane gas. Those are not lakes I'd want to swim in, would you?

Mars, the closest planet to Earth, has long been one of interest for humans. NASA and other scientists have been studying the planet for decades. And despite popular stories of Martians and little green men from space, we have no evidence that life has ever existed on Mars. However, scientists make new discoveries all the time and it is possible tiny lifeforms like microbes once populated the planet.

But so far scientists have not discovered *any* other planets that can support life. The Earth's atmosphere and water conditions are so unique that they are likely very rare elsewhere in the universe, but scientists say it's not impossible! Additionally, humans' ability to explore other planets is still very limited because of how long it takes to travel in space.

Nonetheless, even without the discovery of other plants that can support life, there are many fascinating things in space to learn about and discover!

Chapter Two

The only star in our solar system is the Sun. Even though we can see millions of stars in the sky, the Sun is the only one in our solar system. Not all stars have solar systems - and our solar system is the only one actually called a solar system. But scientists have discovered over 3,900 stars in our galaxy with planets orbiting around them.

If there are that many in just our galaxy, there are likely thousands if not millions more out in the universe! In addition to the sun, planets, and moons, our solar system is also home to dwarf planets, asteroids, and comets.

Dwarf planets are celestial bodies that are round or nearly round but too small to be considered planets and too big to be an asteroid. They often orbit their sun, like Pluto does ours.

Asteroids are small rocky objects that orbit the sun. Most asteroids are very small, but some are as large as 600 miles across; that's over half the width of Texas!

Most asteroids in our solar system live in the asteroid belt between Mars and Jupiter but a few do orbit the Earth. However, we need a telescope to see them! Asteroids are leftover bits of rock from when the solar system formed 4.6 billion years ago.

Comets are similar to asteroids because they orbit the sun. Comets, like asteroids, are ancient and are leftover pieces from the formation of the solar system 4.6 billion years ago - that is a very old piece of ice!

But instead of rock, they are made of ice and dust. Another difference between comets and asteroids is that comets have tails. As a comet's orbit brings it closer to the sun it begins to melt and parts of it evaporate into a gassy, dusty tail. Unlike asteroids, in the right conditions, we can see a comet from Earth.

As a result, people have been interested in them for thousands of years, even when they didn't know what they were!

Chapter Three

Our solar system is part of the galaxy The Milky Way. The galaxy is much bigger than our solar system. Currently, there are almost 4,000 stars discovered with planets orbiting them in The Milky Way, but there are approximately 200 billion stars! Orbiting those nearly 4,000 stars are over 5,000 planets!

Every year scientists discover more solar systems, and they estimate that there are probably tens of billions in our galaxy still undiscovered! Scientists can tell if a star has planets and how many by observing them through very strong telescopes and watching for shadows. If a shadow passes in front of a star at regular intervals, they can assume that it is a planet. They use the size and shape of the shadow to determine how big the planet is.

It is quite amazing that scientists can even discover other planets and stars because the closest stars to us are trillions of light years away! The closest star to our solar system, other than our sun, is called Proxima Centauri. Assuming we could travel at the speed of light, it would take 4.2 years to reach. However, using current technology, it would take 6,300 years to reach!

If we traveled 6,300 years back in human history, that would be to 2,000 years before the Egyptian pyramids were built and around the same time the wheel was invented. That's a long time to travel on a spaceship!

Chapter Four

Beyond our galaxy are other galaxies. Originally scientists were able to observe 5,500 galaxies with the Hubble telescope. But that image only covered 1/32,000,00th of the total universe. Therefore, scientists estimate there are two trillion galaxies in outer space!

And not all galaxies are the same age. There are old galaxies and young galaxies. The furthest observable galaxy outside our own is called GN-z11 and is 13.4 billion years old! By comparison, our galaxy, The Milky Way, is 13.6 billion years old.

The distance a galaxy is from Earth determines how fast light travels. This means even though GN-Z11 is billions of years old, scientists can observe what the galaxy looked like when it was only 600 million years old. That's young for a galaxy!

Every year scientists at NASA and around the world make amazing discoveries about our galaxy and beyond. It is hard to believe we exist in something as large as the universe. Yet here we are! Learning about our solar system, galaxy, and beyond is interesting and creates new questions to be answered.

Reading Comprehension Questions For *Way Up In The Sky: Our Galaxy And Beyond:*

1. Describe what you think it would be like to live on a planet with more than one moon.
2. Have scientists discovered life on other planets yet? Why or why not?
3. What are the similarities and differences between asteroids and comets?
4. Do you think life exists on other planets in the universe? Why or why not?
5. Imagine we could travel at the speed of light and send astronauts to the closest star. What supplies would they need to survive on a spaceship for over four years?
6. List three things you learned about space that you did not know before reading this story.

The Butterfly's Transformation

Chapter One

On a bright green leaf, in a wide, tall, tree, sat a small blue and black caterpillar. The caterpillar hatched from her egg that morning and was curious and hungry. The caterpillar did not know anything yet except that she was a caterpillar. She looked around and saw the bright green leaf she sat upon. Her first thought was, *I'm hungry!* So, she began nibbling the leaf.

She didn't know how she knew to eat the leaf, but her instincts told her to try it. It was delicious! She nibbled more and more until the leaf was gone and she was left sitting on the hard green stem in the middle. The caterpillar was still hungry. She wondered what to do next. As she wondered, she noticed that all around her there were bright green leaves just like the ones she had eaten.

"Why, there are more leaves here than I could possibly ever eat!" She exclaimed. She crawled onto another leaf and began nibbling. The caterpillar ate a second leaf, then a third, and then a fourth! When she reached her fifth leaf, she decided she was tired and wanted a nap.

The little blue and black caterpillar sat on a leaf high in the tree and fell asleep in the warm sun. Her belly was full, and she felt happy and content.

Chapter Two

When the little caterpillar woke up from her nap, she stretched her body out and yawned. She wasn't sure what had happened, but she felt different. As she looked at the leaf she was sitting on, she thought, *this leaf looks smaller.*

But how could the leaf shrink while she was sleeping? That made no sense! She knew she didn't know much about the world, but she was confident she knew that leaves did not shrink! Then she thought, *Oh! Maybe I grew!*

Just as she had this thought, she noticed the leaf above her shaking. The little caterpillar became scared. *Oh, I hope it's not a bird come to eat me!* She thought. She tried to move away as fast as she could, inching her way along the leaf. However, caterpillars don't move very fast, and she had only made it halfway across the leaf when she heard a voice call, "Hello!"

The little caterpillar stopped mid-leaf.

"Hello?" She called back tentatively.

She looked up in the direction of the shaking leaf and the sound of the voice. Over the edge of the leaf, she saw a face that looked similar to hers but bigger. It was another caterpillar! She had never seen another caterpillar. But she had only hatched from her egg four hours ago.

"Hello!" The little caterpillar said again, this time with more energy.

The bigger caterpillar invited her to crawl up to share the leaf he was eating. She was also the first other caterpillar he had seen.

"My, I'm awfully hungry," she said.

"Me too," said the bigger caterpillar. "I hatched from my egg six hours ago and I've eaten four of them!"

The little caterpillar replied, "I hatched four hours ago and ate three of them!"

Both caterpillars laughed.

"I guess that's what caterpillars do," she said. "But I don't know because you're the only other caterpillar I know!"

Chapter Three

The two caterpillars continued to munch leaf after leaf on the big tree. The little caterpillar noticed that the other caterpillar was growing bigger and fatter. She wondered if she was too!

"Excuse me," the little caterpillar said. "But you seem to grow bigger with each leaf you eat. Am I growing too?"

"Of course!" Said the bigger caterpillar. "That's why we eat so much so that we have all the energy we need for our transformation."

"Transformation?" The little caterpillar asked. She had never heard that word before. *What did it mean?*

"Yes!" Said the bigger caterpillar excitedly. "I am not exactly sure what happens, but a big fat caterpillar I met soon after I hatched said he was climbing to the top of the tree to prepare for transformation."

"Oh! I hope it doesn't hurt!" The little caterpillar said.

The bigger caterpillar thought for a moment then replied, "I don't think so. The big, fat caterpillar I met seemed rather excited."

The little caterpillar thought about this. If the big caterpillar said, the *big, fat,* caterpillar he met was excited about the transformation, then surely it must be a good thing!

The two caterpillars continued to eat and nap all day long. The next day, the two friends woke up and continued their feast. Day after day they ate, slept, and grew. Over the week, they met more caterpillars. They talked about the transformation with every caterpillar they met, but none of them knew exactly what to expect.

One caterpillar said, "Maybe to transform means to finally get to the top of the tree!"

Another caterpillar said, "Maybe when we transform, we meet all the other caterpillars!"

A third said, "Maybe to transform means we change color. I've seen caterpillars of different colors eating leaves!"

"Maybe the transformation is a big caterpillar party!" Said a fourth.

The little caterpillar, who was not so little anymore, thought about all of these ideas. Though they all sounded possible, none of them felt right. She really wanted to learn what the transformation was!

Chapter Four

After nearly a month of eating, sleeping, and growing fatter, the little caterpillar had a feeling she was supposed to make something. But she wasn't sure what she was supposed to make! She asked the other caterpillars if they felt the same instinct, and they all agreed but no one could agree on what to make.

One caterpillar said they felt like they were supposed to make a house of some type. Another argued they felt the need to make a blanket. A third said it was a sweater they were supposed to make! As the caterpillars argued back and forth about what they were supposed to make, a beautiful butterfly landed on the leaf next to them.

"Hello, caterpillars!" She said in a cheerful and loud voice.

The caterpillars all turned to look at the butterfly. She had large silky wings that were black and streaked with silvery-blue lines. The butterfly had two long and graceful antennas and long graceful legs.

The caterpillars all stared at her in amazement. A butterfly had never spoken to them before!

"I am here to teach you about your transformation! You will all be ready in another day or two!"

The caterpillars became very excited; wow, finally they would learn what it meant to transform!

The butterfly explained that, after their transformation, they would be a butterfly just like her.

The little caterpillar couldn't believe it. How could she possibly turn into something as beautiful and graceful as a butterfly?

"Each of you will find a sturdy branch on this tree and create your chrysalis. You will use a silky pad to attach yourself to the branch. Make sure you choose a strong branch because you will be inside your chrysalis for several weeks!"

"Several weeks!" The caterpillars all cried out.

"Yes," said the butterfly, "that is why you've been eating so much, to ensure you have enough energy for your transformation!"

The butterfly continued explaining how they would shed their skin to create their chrysalis and then while inside transform into a butterfly. It seemed impossible to believe. The little caterpillar was worried at first that the butterfly was teasing them. But the more the butterfly told them about the transformation, the more the little caterpillar could feel it was true.

Now the little caterpillar was becoming quite excited! The butterfly told them they would feel when it was the right time to attach to their branch and to be ready any day now!

Chapter Five

The very next morning, the little caterpillar woke knowing today was the day she would form her chrysalis. She said goodbye to the other caterpillars and went out in search of the perfect, sturdy branch.

The little caterpillar climbed high and deep into the tree until she found a perfect spot! She attached herself to the branch and began shedding her skin to make her chrysalis. In a way, her and the other caterpillars' instincts were correct. A chrysalis was kind of like a home, a blanket, and a sweater all in one!

She still had a hard time believing that she would emerge a beautiful butterfly, but she was also very excited! Once her chrysalis was formed, the little caterpillar fell into a deep sleep.

She stayed in a deep sleep for many days and nights.

Then one morning she woke up. The little caterpillar was confused when she first woke up. *Where am I? Why do I feel so different?* Then slowly she began to remember about the transformation and the chrysalis and that she wasn't a caterpillar anymore!

She started to stretch and push, and her chrysalis popped open and so did her wings. Wings! She had wings now, she was a butterfly! She looked at her silky blue and black wings and stretched her elegant long legs. She flapped her wings a few times and slowly began to hover in the air. She was flying!

What a wonderful feeling. She flew from her tree to a beautiful flower bush and began drinking the nectar. She thought the nectar tasted much better than the leaves she ate as a caterpillar.

The little caterpillar, now a beautiful butterfly, was amazed by her transformation but also very happy. What a wonderful world to live in where little caterpillars could transform into amazing and lovely butterflies.

Reading Comprehension Questions For *The Butterfly's Transformation*:

1. The story tells us that the caterpillar's "instincts" told her to eat the leaf. What do you think the word "instincts" means?
2. How did the two caterpillars feel when they met each other? Why?
3. How did the little caterpillar feel about the transformation before she knew what it was?
4. What did the little caterpillar have to do to transform?
5. How did the little caterpillar feel after her transformation?

The Music That Makes Me Dance

Chapter One

I love all types of music. I listen to music every day and as much of the day as possible. I love music so much that my mom calls me a music maniac! My day starts with music. My alarm clock plays Beethoven's 5th Symphony. It never fails to wake me up and energize me for the day ahead. I love the big sound of classical symphonies. I think it is amazing how so many instruments can play at once and sound wonderful!

My big brother Benji thinks I'm odd for waking up to classical music. But I think he's odd for wanting to race pretend cars on a computer screen all day. I guess to each their own.

Once I'm awake, I play music while I get ready for school. Some mornings I listen to jazz, and other mornings pop, but my favorite morning music is rock and roll.

Next to classical, I love rock and roll the best! But each type of music has a special place in my heart, so even though I really love classical music and rock and roll, I love all types of music.

During my bus ride to school, I use my headphones and listen to music that prepares me for the day. My best friend Josie rides a different bus, so I usually prefer listening to music over talking to the other kids, but not always.

I find that music by Schubert or Chopin is excellent music to prepare my brain for school. Schubert and Chopin are classical music too, but their music is calmer than Beethoven's 5th symphony; it's more melody-focused, I think.

But every once in a while, I get into a phase where I listen to something completely different.

For example, two weeks ago we learned about bluegrass in music class, and for a week I listened to nothing but banjo music on my bus ride each morning.

Banjo and bluegrass music is lively and jaunty and makes me want to tap my toes!

And speaking of tapping my toes, I don't only like listening to music; I also love to dance!

Chapter Two

Dancing is my favorite hobby. I take three different dance classes! I have tap class on Monday nights, jazz on Thursday nights, and ballet on Saturday mornings.

I dance so much my dad says I have a dancing fever!

But I love to dance to more than just tap, jazz, and ballet. I also love modern dance! They just started a modern dance club at my school, and Mom said I could sign up for the club.

Modern dance is great because it combines unique and different moves and styles of dance.

I like to watch modern dance videos at home and try to copy them.

My brother saw me in my room once trying out some modern dance steps and he said I looked like a flamingo who was ill. But what does he know?

All he does is play video games and talk to his friends on the phone.

Maybe I was wearing hot pink like a flamingo, but I definitely think I looked cool no matter what Benji said!

That's what makes dance and music so great!

There are so many ways to express yourself creatively that even if you play a wrong note or take a wrong step if you do it with passion, you're not really wrong! At least that's what my dance teacher, Ms. Chloe, tells us.

Ms. Chloe says she'd rather have us make a big mistake with passion than be perfect but have zero passion. I am not so sure my piano teacher Mrs. Ruebens feels the same way because when I make a mistake, she makes me play the section until I play it five times in a row with no mistakes. But I guess not everyone can have the same opinion!

I love modern dance. I love jazz, tap, and ballet. But there is one type of music that really gets me dancing, but I've never shared it with anyone. It's kind of my little dancing secret!

Chapter Three

The type of music that really makes me want to get up and dance is country line music! I know, it probably sounds crazy. I'm not from the south or west. In fact, I am a very typical, northeast suburban kid. But I secretly love country line dancing.

I've never told anyone. Not my mom. Not my dad. And definitely not Benji. He already teases me about enough things! I haven't even confided my dancing secret to my best friend Josie. I don't know why I haven't told her. I guess I'm worried she'll tease me; she's always said she *hates* country music.

But I'm not sure if Josie really dislikes country music or only says that because her really popular and cool older sister Savannah does. Josie likes music and dance; she's in my tap class with me, but she doesn't love it the way I do.

We have so many other things in common that we don't talk about music that much. We both love penguins, the color green, cheeseburger mac n' cheese, P.E. class, and the movies *Shrek* and *Tangled.*

Some days I come really close to telling Josie about my love of country line dancing, but something always stops me. Maybe I have to face the fear of telling her. After all, if she is truly my best friend then she may tease me *a little,* but she'd still be my best friend. I don't think I have ever heard of a friendship ending over country music.

Chapter Four

Today is Sunday and Sunday is one of my favorite days of the week. I don't have school or any classes or lessons. I can hang out in my room and listen to music or hang out with Josie if she's around. I like to read books on Sunday afternoons and sometimes I help my mom or dad cook dinner.

But my very favorite thing about Sunday is that I usually have time to myself to secretly practice my country line dancing. I usually play music in my headphones so no one else in the house can hear me, and I lock my door so no one can come in. I started closing my door when I danced after my brother called me an ill flamingo. I don't need to be compared to any other injured or sick animals!

I have no plans this afternoon and Josie said she was going to be out shopping with her mom, so it's the perfect time to practice! I put on my sparkly cowboy boots and hat I purchased from the local theater's costume sale. I pull up my country line dance playlist and scroll through the songs.

There's "Boot Scootin' Boogie" or "Achy Breaky Heart," or my favorite, "Man! I Feel Like a Woman." I scroll through a few more songs but then decide on "Boot Scootin' Boogie" for my first dance today!

I connect my Bluetooth headphones, push play on my music, and start dancing. What I love about country line dancing is the upbeat playfulness of the music. To me, it's impossible to *not* dance when you hear such fun music!

I am in the middle of getting my boogie on when my door opens, only I don't hear it. I keep dancing. Then as I turn, I see Josie standing in my doorway with her mouth hanging wide open - I forgot to lock my door!

Chapter Five

I quickly stop the music, remove my headphones, and ask Josie what she's doing here. Josie told me shopping with her mom ended early, so she asked her mom to drop her off here to surprise me. Well, it worked! I was *very* surprised!

Josie asks me what I am wearing and what I am doing, so I decide it's time to tell the truth. I confess to Josie my secret love of country music and how country line dancing is the music that truly makes me want to dance. Josie is quiet and listens to me and then tells me the most shocking thing!

She tells me that she *also* secretly loves country music. Now it is my turn to stare with my mouth open wide. I tell her I'm so confused because she always says she hates country music.

Josie tells me she only says that so Savannah won't tease her. Because I never said anything, she thought I hated it too! Of all the secrets and surprises, I could have learned about my best friend, I never thought it would be that she loved country music as much as me!

We enjoy a good laugh over our shared secret and then I ask her if she wants to dance. She says yes! This time, I play the music loudly. I don't care who knows if I like country line music and dancing. I realize it is a silly thing to keep a secret. My love of ALL music is part of what makes me, me!

Reading Comprehension Questions For *The Music That Makes Me Dance*:

1. Why does the narrator say they like classical symphonies?
2. The narrator tells us their dance teacher says it's better to make mistakes with passion than to be perfect with zero passion. What do you think she means? Do you agree? Why or why not?
3. Do you think the author of the story is a girl or a boy? Why? What context clues support your answer?
4. Why is the narrator afraid to tell Josie they like country line dancing? What happened when Josie found out?
5. Do you think the narrator is correct that it shouldn't matter what type of music you like? Why or why not?

Working On The Railroad: A Story Of Chinese American Immigrants

Chapter One

Henry Chang was in his grandmother's attic on a rainy Saturday afternoon. Usually, when Henry visited his grandmother with his parents, he would play outside. Today there was nothing but pouring rain. Henry's grandmother, Li Na, had told him there were some boxes in the attic with old toys and games and sent him upstairs to look.

Nothing was labeled, so Henry began opening boxes randomly in search of a game to play with his parents and grandmother. So far Henry had found books, clothing, a box of dishes, and even an entire box of old shoes! But no games yet.

Henry opened another box and a puff of dust hit him in the face, making him sneeze. When he looked down at the open box, he saw a stack of old postcards tied together and underneath them an old photo album.

Interested, Henry pulled the photo album out of the box and opened it. Henry's grandmother had many old pictures framed in her house, but he had never seen these photos before. These photos looked very old. The farther back in the album he went, the older the photos looked.

Henry didn't recognize any of the people or places in the photos, but he assumed most of them were in San Francisco where he was born. He knew both his parents were also born in San Francisco, but he wasn't sure about his grandmother.

There was one photo in the very back that was black and white. There were a few men in old-fashioned clothes standing on and next to a piece of equipment. They looked like they were on train tracks.

Henry decided he would take the photo album downstairs and ask his grandmother about the photo.

Henry approached his grandmother with the album and asked her about the photo in the back.

"Ah," his grandmother said, pointing to a young-looking man standing toward the front, "that is my great-great-grandfather, Yuze. He is half the reason our family lives in America!"

"Half?" Henry questioned.

"Yes, my great-great-grandmother is the other half!" She said, laughing at her joke.

"Why did they come here?" Henry asked.

Henry's grandmother said, "That is an excellent story! Let me tell you the history of your family." And she settled into a fantastic but true tale of the early Chinese immigrants to America.

Chapter Two

"My great-great-grandfather Yuze came to America because there was work here," Henry's grandmother began, "and it was a chance to try and make it big with the American dream. Back then every immigrant, whether Irish, Italian, Chinese, Jewish, etc., thought they would make lots of money here."

"Yuze arrived on a boat in 1864. His cousin Bao had come the year before and told him there was going to be work on a new American railroad! Yuze was not married, both his parents had died, and he had no brothers and sisters, so he decided he would give America a chance.

"He was young, only 19 years old! Can you imagine taking such a big trip at such a young age? Why that's only nine years older than you are! But Yuze was brave and wanted adventure, so he came.

"He was lucky, in a way, he found one of the earliest jobs on the Central Pacific railroad, but the pay was terrible, and the work was hard. But he and Bao, that's the man next to him, were working together and chose to stay.

"More and more Chinese men came to America to help build the railroad, but work conditions did not improve. So, the men held a strike. Do you know what a strike is?"

Henry shook his head, no. Then his grandmother continued.

"A strike is when people refuse to work until their pay or conditions are better.

"These men were brave to strike, especially being immigrants. But it worked! Their conditions *did* improve even if their pay did not! The work was finally completed two years later and Yuze, like many Chinese immigrants stayed in California.

"It's a good thing too because that is where he met my great-great-grandmother Li Jing!"

Henry's grandmother flipped to another page and showed him a photograph of a young woman standing outside a house.

Chapter Three

"After the railroad was completed," Henry's grandmother continued, "Yuze found work at the railyards unloading cargo when trains arrived. It was hard work, but he was strong from his years on the railroad, and he was still very young.

"Every night after he finished working, he would go home to his boarding house where his landlady and her husband would have dinner prepared. One night, very tired and sore, he sat down to eat, and a young woman brought him his food.

"Can you guess who it was? It was Li Jing! She was the landlady's granddaughter from her first marriage, and she had just arrived in America. The landlady was getting older and said she needed help, so she sent for her only granddaughter.

"According to my grandmother, Li Jang, and Yuze's granddaughter, he fell in love at first sight! But I don't know if such a thing exists. But night after night my grandfather looked for Li Jing to bring him his dinner.

"He was very shy, my grandmother says, but after several weeks he began talking to her. He asked her about her home in China and her family. My great-great-grandmother was a little lonely in America, so she enjoyed having someone her age to talk to.

"At the time, most of the Chinese immigrants in America were men because of the jobs available. Very few women came, unless, like her grandmother, they were married to a merchant. She did not have any friends here, so Yuze quickly became her friend.

"Over the following months, they talked almost nightly and realized they had many things in common. I do not know if my great-great-grandparents would have fallen in love if there were more choices of people their age, but I like to think that they would have!"

Chapter Four

"My great-great-grandfather continued to work for the railroad as long as he was able," Henry's grandmother said, as Henry listened intently. "But eventually, he became too old for the work. But he always loved the railway and passed that love down to his son, and he passed it to my grandmother, and to my mother and to me!"

"I love trains, too!" Henry said.

"See?" His grandmother said. "It runs in the family!"

"So, what happened after he stopped working at the shipyard?" Henry asked.

"Well, by then he and Li Jing owned the boarding house he used to stay at, and they owned two other ones too!" His grandmother explained.

"Isn't a boarding house like a hotel?" Henry asked.

"Exactly!" Said his grandmother.

"Wait," said Henry, "is that why we own a hotel now?"

"Yes!" His grandmother exclaimed. "I was wondering when you would solve that puzzle. Yuze and Li Jing passed three boarding houses down to my great-grandparents. Then, by the time I was a little girl in the 1950s, my grandparents owned six boarding houses!

"It was your grandfather and I who bought the hotel that your parents now run."

"But what happened to the boarding houses?" Henry asked.

"Oh, we sold three of them. One is now an apartment building for rental, and the other two are bed and breakfasts. A bed and breakfast place is sort of like a hotel, but smaller and feels more like a home," his grandmother explained.

"Wow. I had no idea our family history was so interesting!" Henry said.

"I have many more stories I can tell you, any time you'd like! Now bring that picture album over here and let's take a look at some more photos."

Reading Comprehension Questions For *Working On The Railroad: A Story Of Chinese American Immigrants:*

1. Why was Henry in the attic?
2. Why was Henry's grandmother's great-great-grandmother lonely when she first came to America?
3. What did the railroad workers do when they wanted better working conditions and pay? Did it work? Why or why not?
4. What was Henry surprised to discover about his family's history?
5. How do you think Henry's grandmother felt telling Henry the story? Why?
6. Ask your parents to tell you a story about your family history!

Conclusion

We hope you enjoyed these fun and uniquely crafted stories for fourth-grade readers. Each story was broken into small chapters to assist with reading comprehension. While these chapters are much shorter than a standard book chapter, they were designed this way to help focus on reading comprehension, memory, and retention. You may already be reading some books with lengthier chapters and several pages long! Our small chapters mimic the style of longer chapter books, but we kept them short to help young readers.

Each of the stories in this book uses common sight words and words fourth-grade level readers will recognize or can decipher using context clues. But there are also some new and challenging or unfamiliar words to help push you to the next level! Remember, it is OK if you do not know how to say a word or what it means. Reading and hearing new words is how you learn them.

But stories do much more than teach words. Stories engage your imagination and teach you to dream of new and exciting things. Stories teach us about new people and places and help us learn about ourselves too. Some stories evoke adventure, some teach valuable lessons about family and friendship, while others are simply fun to read!

When you read a story, it opens windows to new ways of thinking. They help you learn something new about yourself and about those with whom you share the world. What did you learn while reading these stories? Did you discover anything new about yourself or someone you may know? Do you have a favorite story in the book? Which one and why?

We encourage you to read your favorites again and again! Just like watching your favorite movie over and over it is an awesome idea to re-read your favorite stories. The more you read a story, the more familiar the words become, the faster your flow becomes, and the more you comprehend or understand.

In addition to language and literacy skills, reading promotes problem-solving and other cognitive skills. That is why each story includes a set of reading comprehension and thought-provoking questions at the end.

While these stories are designed for fourth-grade readers (ages eight to ten), older and younger children will enjoy them too!

We also encourage you to use the guided reading questions at the beginning of this book, which can be applied to any story in the book to enhance your reading and comprehension skills.

Made in the USA
Las Vegas, NV
03 December 2024